Tucker

LITTLE DOG LOST & FOUND

by Danny Sit

STERLING

New York / London

Dedicated to a special Jack Russell
who taught me about love.

STERLING and the distinctive Sterling logo are
registered trademarks of Sterling Publishing Co., Inc.

Library of Congress Cataloging-in-Publication Data Available

Lot #:
10 9 8 7 6 5 4 3 2

04/11

Published by Sterling Publishing Co., Inc.
387 Park Avenue South, New York, NY 10016
© 2011 by Danny Sit
Distributed in Canada by Sterling Publishing
c/o Canadian Manda Group, 165 Dufferin Street
Toronto, Ontario, Canada M6K 3H6
Distributed in the United Kingdom by GMC Distribution Services
Castle Place, 166 High Street, Lewes, East Sussex, England BN7 1XU
Distributed in Australia by Capricorn Link (Australia) Pty. Ltd.
P.O. Box 704, Windsor, NSW 2756, Australia

Printed in China
All rights reserved

Sterling ISBN 978-1-4027-5999-4

For information about custom editions, special sales, premium and
corporate purchases, please contact Sterling Special Sales
Department at 800-805-5489 or specialsales@sterlingpublishing.com.

Credits
Storyline/Concept by Suzanne Bressler
Photography by Danny Sit
Written by Danny Sit
First rough edit by Dan Milch
Art Direction/Production by Liz Long
Design layout by Lisa Maione/Merideth Harte

My name is Tucker with a capital "T."

When I woke up today, I had no idea
what the day would bring.

The bed called out, "Don't go."
But I pretended that I didn't hear.

I greeted Turtle, my favorite toy,
as I always do.

"Today," I announced to Turtle,
"I'm going on an adventure!"

All through breakfast I thought about how much fun my adventure would be.

But where would I go?

I was so busy thinking that I forgot to help clean up. Papa didn't seem to notice. He told me I was the best little dog in the whole wide world, so I gave him a big wet kiss right on his nose.

I thought so hard that after a while
my head felt heavy. Since napping is my
favorite thing to do and there's
no time like the present, it was off to
dreamland for me.

After my nap I climbed to the tallest tree in the yard. I looked north, south, east and west.

But I still couldn't decide where to go.

I wondered if packing would help me figure it out.

First, I packed my new coat with the fancy dog tag.

Papa said the tag would come in handy if I ever got in trouble.

It was a warm and sunny day, but Papa always says that the weather can change in the blink of an eye.

What if it got chilly?

I even imagined that an iceberg floated down from the North Pole, and I was stranded on it.

Just in case, I'd bring my warmest sweater.

Then I imagined
that there was a
big rainstorm.

Jack Russells don't
like rain, so I packed
my yellow raincoat.

I imagined some fun
stuff too.

What if a cool rock band
asked me to join?

Just in case, I packed
my favorite hoodie.

Taking a ride in Papa's car was
always a lot of fun —
besides being comfy!
I hopped right in to get going
on my adventure.

But the car was too big for a
little dog like me. I couldn't even
reach the pedals.

"Now what?" I asked.
"How am I going to begin
my adventure?"

I remembered that Papa went to work each day on a train.

Maybe I could take a train just like he did. I ran as fast as I could to the station.

Just then the
train pulled in
and the station-
master bellowed,
"ALL ABOARD."

I hopped right on
the train, even
though I didn't know
where it was going.
The conductor even
got me a seat
by the window.
"Hot diggity dog!"
I thought, and
settled in for a
little nap.

I woke up when a
whistle blew "TOOT"
and the train screeched
to a stop. I jumped off, and
as soon as I did my nose
and my ears told me
where my adventure
had led me.

"I can smell the
ocean," I sang.
"I can smell the
sea. I am just a little
dog, but I'm happy
as can be!"

I ran to the edge of the water.
The rocks felt good on my back,
and the sun felt good on my tummy.

I gathered some driftwood.

I dug some clams.

"How many biscuits can
I trade for a bucket of clams?"
I wondered.

Lucky little dog that
I am, I even found
a big blue ball that
some other dog had
left behind.

"Life's good!"
I said to myself.
I was just about
to have a picnic,
but something
stopped me in
my tracks:

I was all alone, and
I didn't know how
to find my way
back home.

Where is my bed?
Where is Turtle?
And where is Papa?

I ran up and down the
beach looking for them.

I remembered the day Papa
brought me home.

What fun we had!

I remembered the time I hurt my paw and how
our cat Eloise took special care of me.

I sat down on the
beach and howled
and howled.
"I'm lost!"

Suddenly, I heard a
familiar bark and I
spied my best friend,
Puddles, walking
down the beach.

"I'm lost," I cried. "I'm lost and I can't find Papa!"

"Calm down," Puddles said.

"Help me bring this stick to my mommy, and I'm sure she'll help you find Papa."

Puddles's mommy, whom we call Two Legs, picked me up and gave me a great big hug. Gee, that was swell.

Two Legs showed me a picture. It looked very familiar. "Who is this little dog?" I wondered.

"It's a picture of YOU, silly," she said. "Papa's been posting these everywhere. You'd better come home with us."

So, off we went.

As soon as we got there,
I started to feel better.

"What about naps?"
I asked.

"Is there naptime here?"

As nice as it
was at Puddles's
home, it still wasn't
my home. And I
still missed Papa.

But then the door opened,
and there he was!

"Tucker, oh Tucker," Papa said.
"Where have you been?"

I told him everything. I was so happy I
gave kisses to everyone!

Mostly on their ankles. After all,
I am a very little dog.

It took a while to
settle down.
Finally (and this is
the best part)
we headed HOME!

My adventure today was tons of fun. But when it's all been said and done, near family and friends is the place to be. And there's nothing more fun than just being me — that's Tucker with a capital "T."

Danny lives in Southampton with two Jack Russells, Apple and Henri. They take frequent naps, but mostly at night.

ACKNOWLEDGMENTS
With thanks to Liz Long, whose persistence, production, and unwavering support was instrumental from start to finish; Suzanne Bressler, who painstakingly organized thousands of photographs into a darling story concept; Mary Sit, whose journalistic background gave shape to my novice writing skills; Eva Whitechapel, who took time from writing her own book to allow me to tap into her artistic views; Suzanne Lee, for her logical, no-nonsense critique; Garrick Doldberg and Elisa Amorosa, for graphic and copy advice (keep it simple); Bubba, who contributed his wit and humor for some great one-liners; Cookie Carosella, who suggested the lost dog concept; Barbara Berger, who got my rough draft in front of the right people; Bill Luckey, who accepted this book at Sterling Children's Books; and, of course, my agent, Jennifer DeChiara, for believing in me and rescuing me from the slush pile. Lastly, a heartfelt tribute to my dog Barney, whose personality inspired this book.